Praise for Maeve Binchy

'One of the world's best-loved writers'
Woman's Weekly

'Binchy weaves her magic once again in an
addictive story about families and people who
aren't always quite what they seem'
Woman & Home

'It's little wonder that Maeve Binchy's
bewitching stories have become world-beaters'
OK! Magazine

'Make no mistake, there is magic at work'
Sunday Times

'Once you read Maeve you are hooked for life'
Irish Times

'A Maeve classic, it'll leave a warm, fuzzy
feeling in your tummy' *Company*

'An absolute delight from the most loved of
storytellers' *My Weekly*

By Maeve Binchy

Fiction
Light a Penny Candle
Echoes
The Lilac Bus
Firefly Summer
Silver Wedding
Circle of Friends
The Copper Beech
The Glass Lake
Evening Class
Tara Road
Scarlet Feather
Quentins
Nights of Rain and Stars
Star Sullivan (Quick Read)
Whitethorn Woods
Heart and Soul
Minding Frankie
A Week in Winter

Non-fiction
Aches & Pains
The Maeve Binchy Writers' Club
Maeve's Times

Short Stories
Victoria Line, Central Line
Dublin 4
This Year It Will Be Different
The Return Journey

Maeve Binchy was born in County Dublin and educated at the Holy Child convent in Killiney and at University College, Dublin. After a spell as a teacher she joined the *Irish Times*. Her first novel, *Light a Penny Candle*, was published in 1982 and she went on to write over twenty books, all of them bestsellers. Several have been adapted for cinema and television, most notably *Circle of Friends* and *Tara Road*. Maeve Binchy received a Lifetime Achievement Award at the British Book Awards in 1999 and the Irish PEN/A.T. Cross Award in 2007. In 2010 she was presented with the Bob Hughes Lifetime Achievement Award at the Bord Gáis Irish Book Awards by the President of Ireland. Maeve also won the Popular Fiction Prize at the 2012 Bord Gáis Irish Book Awards for her last novel, *A Week in Winter*. She was married to the writer and broadcaster Gordon Snell for 35 years, and died in 2012. Visit her website at www.maevebinchy.com

Full House

Maeve Binchy

An Orion paperback

First published in Great Britain in 2012
by Orion Books Ltd,
Orion House, 5 Upper St Martin's Lane,
London WC2H 9EA

An Hachette UK company

16

A CIP catalogue record for this book
is available from the British Library.

ISBN 978 1 4091 3661 3

Typeset at The Spartan Press Ltd,
Lymington, Hants

Printed and bound in Great Britain by Clays Ltd,
St Ives plc

The Orion Publishing Group's policy is to use papers that
are natural, renewable and recyclable products and made
from wood grown in sustainable forests. The logging and
manufacturing processes are expected to conform to the
environmental regulations of the country of origin.

Distributed By:
Grass Roots Press
Toll Free: 1-888-303-3213
Fax: (780) 413-6582
Web Site: www.grassrootsbooks.net

For dearest Gordon,
the kindest man on earth.

Chapter One

It had been a long day for Dee Nolan. Up at four in the morning and a quick clear-up of the kitchen, then down to the end of St Jarlath's Crescent to wait for Josie. Josie had a van and would come by at four-thirty on the dot. The van was full of vacuums and cleaning materials.

Josie and Dee were J.D. Contract Cleaners.

From five to seven they cleaned offices. Then they went to apartment blocks and did halls, stairs and landings. Dee liked that, they weren't messy like the offices that she had to clean. It was only a question of running a Dyson over a smooth thick carpet and wiping the skirting boards.

Josie would sing old music-hall songs to herself, it helped the hours go by. Dee would clean on cheerfully and imagine to herself what it must be like to live or work in the places she cleaned.

Sometimes she knew what it was like to live in such comfort because J.D. Contract Cleaners did work in people's homes from nine to one o'clock. They had more keys than a jailer, and they found the places in varying degrees of mess. Like that woman Sonia, who was a real tramp. Her clothes were all over the place. They had once found her bra up on the light shade. She always left wet towels in a puddle on the bathroom floor. She seemed to eat food all over the house, there were dirty plates in every room.

She also left little notes.

Ladies

Please be sweethearts and take all the dirty sheets and things to the launderette down the road for a service wash. Thank you so much, you are such angels . . .

She had never seen them, met them, thanked them, or bought them a Christmas drink. The money was paid by a direct debit from the bank. There must be rich parents somewhere. Some people had it very easy.

Then there was Miss Mason. She cleaned up before the cleaners arrived. They could spend real time polishing up her lovely sideboard until it gleamed, then arranging her glassware on it. Miss Mason was retired and lonely, and she loved the chat as much – if not more than –

10

the cleaning. She knew all about Dee's husband, Liam, and the three children, Rosie, Anthony and Helen. And she knew all about Josie's husband, Harry, who played in a band, and the dog Pepper who was the light of Josie's life.

There were other people they worked for who were almost unknown. There was that one who was on television. People would be very surprised if they knew how many vodka bottles Josie and Dee took from *her* apartment to the recycling bin . . .

That was eight hours' cleaning work a day. And at the minimum wage. It didn't matter that they had a van and business cards with the name of a company on them. Other people would call to doors and offer their cleaning services at a cheaper rate. Customers were always anxious to get things cheaper, even people who lived in really expensive places.

Dee wondered about that. If she ever had a lot of money, she would be generous, pay people much higher than the minimum wage, encourage them. Or maybe she only thought that now . . .

At one o'clock Josie and Dee would go to the cut-price supermarket and fill a bag with bargains. Then they would have a bowl of soup and a sandwich in a grand cheap place that they had found. Two small, blonde, cheerful forty-somethings. People would often smile at them and call them over to join a group. But Josie and Dee had no time for such delays. They were both keen to get home. Their day wasn't nearly over yet. They would just laugh, wave goodbye and climb into the van.

Josie would drop Dee at the end of St Jarlath's Crescent and then drive back home to walk Pepper round the park. She'd prepare some simple supper that Harry could eat whatever time he returned from whatever his musical career had called him to this time. And Dee would walk down her road to a full house.

They hadn't intended it to be a full house. Dee and Liam had thought that their children would leave home one by one and come to see them at weekends. It had started out fairly normally: Rosie got married at the age of twenty-two. But now at twenty-five she said the marriage was over, that Ronan was a pig. She was back in St Jarlath's Crescent, her home that she never should have left.

She shared the bedroom as before with her sister Helen, who was a teacher. Helen had never left home. She was a dreamy girl, full of ideals and hopes. There was nothing that she wasn't going to do for her pupils.

Anthony had left home for a year when he went around the world like everyone did or should. He was amazed that his mother had never been to Cambodia and his father hadn't made it to Australia. Anthony was a musician. He wrote his own songs, which he accompanied on his guitar. Hour after hour they heard him at the kitchen table or in his room uploading them on to YouTube. One day, someone somewhere would hear one of his songs. That's how all the greats were discovered.

She loved them all, who wouldn't love their three children? But there were times like today when she could have done with coming home to a quiet house. Maybe put her feet up for a while until Liam came in and brought her a mug of tea. There would be no time for anything like that.

Dee Nolan, who had spent eight hours cleaning other people's places, would have to make a start on her own.

At four-thirty this morning, Dee had glimpsed a big bundle of clothes beside the washing machine. Clean, she thought, so that would mean ironing. She needed to give the fridge a bit of a clear-out before putting in all the low-fat yoghurt that was the Bargain of the Week. She had got a piece of lamb to make an Irish stew, she would have to cut that up and slice the vegetables. That left very little time to put her feet up and have a mug of tea.

She saluted her neighbours as she headed for number sixteen.

Noel and Faith Lynch were at their garden gate. They had recently bought a house in the street just down from Noel's parents. Their little girl, Frankie, was playing at the railings. Dee wondered whether Frankie would still be living there in twenty years' time. Would her parents, like so many, never experience the strangeness but the peace of an empty nest?

Dee passed Lizzie Scarlett's house. Lizzie wasn't home. She worked day shifts in Ennio's restaurant, where her granddaughter was engaged to the son of the house, Marco. Dee had known Lizzie forever and, in the years since her husband Muttie died, Lizzie had lived quietly on her own. There would be plenty of time in that household for a feet-up and a mug of tea, Dee thought wistfully. Lizzie's children were all settled in their own homes and didn't expect her to run around after them.

In her own house everyone was sitting around the kitchen table. It was covered with dishes. They must have all gathered for lunch. The saucepan might have held pasta, there was a ring of tomato sauce dried on it. It had dripped on to the hob and the burned bits would have to be scraped off.

Dee could see they had eaten the apple tart that she had been planning for the evening meal. There was no milk left. There had been at least a litre there this morning. There was an empty wrapper from a packet of biscuits.

'How's everyone?' she asked brightly through gritted teeth.

'Well for you, Mam, work finished for the day.'

Rosie must have come home on a late lunch break. She worked in a shopping centre doing free make ups for clients. She would target women likely to buy the cosmetics and apply foundation, blusher and eye shadow. They got a percentage of what the customers paid for the products. It wasn't a proper living. They would have to convince a lot of women about the worth of tawny this or shiny that before they could bring home a decent wage.

'Poor Mam got up very early when we were all asleep,' Helen said, reaching out to take the last biscuit. Dee saw that the teapot was empty.

'Teachers have it made,' Rosie grumbled.

15

'Months of holiday every year and home in the middle of the afternoon.'

Anthony had obviously eaten some lunch too; there was an empty plate with a knife and fork on it. As usual, all she could see of Anthony was the top of his head as he bent over his iPod or whatever it was. Dee had seen a lot of Anthony's head and his hair parting over the past couple of years. She had addressed questions to it and reminded it to put its dirty clothes into the washing machine. She suggested that it might apply itself more frequently to tidying up the garden, or painting the hall door. Always Anthony's head would nod eagerly in agreement, but his eyes never left the small screen in front of him.

Dee felt very tired. She sat down at the kitchen table. Liam got up to get her some fresh tea. There was something in the way he moved that alarmed her. He was walking very slowly. There was a sense that he was taking every action very seriously, filling the kettle, rinsing the teapot.

'You're home early, Liam?' she said.

She hoped he hadn't felt sick or anything and left before the working day was over. He had a great job as an electrician for Mash Macken, a small builder. Liam had worked with Mash for nearly twenty years. It was a solid firm, a good job, working with decent people.

She watched his strange, soldier-like movements with increasing concern.

'Mash let us all go at two o'clock. He's buying us a drink at seven, so I won't be in for supper,' he said.

'A drink? In the middle of the week?' Dee was surprised.

'That's what he said.' Liam was tight-lipped.

None of the children seemed to notice that anything was wrong. Rosie was yawning and examining her already flawless face in a magnifying mirror. Helen had her part of the table spread with brochures of Paris: she was planning a school outing. Anthony was concentrating on his texting.

'Maybe you'd bring it upstairs to me, Liam,' Dee said. At least in their bedroom they could talk.

He nodded and put two mugs on a tray.

She didn't even wait to unpack her shopping. So what if the yoghurt should go straight into the fridge, the bread into the big airtight tin. The biscuits should be put into the plastic box where they would remain for the next ten minutes until someone downstairs wanted one.

Upstairs in the bedroom that looked out on

the street, they sat in the two little chairs with the round table between them. When Dee was young her mother had said that a table with a cloth over it was the height of class in a bedroom. Especially the Master Bedroom. People still used that word to describe the front bedroom. Dee and Liam would laugh at it. Nothing very masterful about their room.

There was a big bed with built-in cupboards on either side. There were suitcases for holidays that they didn't take any more, and Dee's salsa dress for dance classes she didn't go to nowadays. She was too tired for one thing and they were too dear for another.

On the wall was a poster of Taormina in Sicily where they had spent their honeymoon and a Spanish hat they had bought in Majorca when they had the family holiday there long ago. It always made them laugh.

Today they didn't laugh as they sipped their tea. They both looked troubled.

'What is it, Liam?' Dee asked eventually.

'It's Mash. He's gone. The whole thing is over.' His face looked bleak and empty.

'Mash Macken in trouble? I don't believe it. Hasn't he a load of work?'

'Had. But people aren't paying him. Because

of the downturn. You know those fourteen townhouses we did?'

'I do, weren't they marvellous?'

'Yes, but not any more. The guy who developed them is skint. He ran off to England and left a letter for Mash saying he was sorry. Sorry? That was what we were all relying on.'

'Didn't Mash get any money in advance, like a deposit? Or anything?' Dee felt a cold lump beginning to form inside.

'You know the way it is. Mash told us straight. This guy put so much business his way and always paid up before. It would be like spitting in his face to ask him for a deposit.'

'And now look what's happened. Will he be letting people go, or giving short hours to everyone?' Dee searched his face for the answer. But she didn't need to search any longer.

'He's paying us off tonight, and he's going to sell whatever stuff he has around the yard and divide it up. It won't get much, nobody's building now. And then he's off to live with his daughter in Australia.'

'And . . . ?' Dee could barely speak.

'And we're all on the scrap heap, Dee. As from tomorrow I'm unemployed.'

Chapter Two

'Mam and Dad are a long time upstairs,' Helen said as she looked up from her brochures.

'They're probably at it,' Rosie said, sighing with disapproval.

'Rosie!' Helen was horrified. 'Come on! They're much too old.'

'Men never think that, they want to do it every single night.' Rosie spoke with the voice of authority.

'But Rosie, it's not the same. Ronan is young, but Dad . . . I mean, can you imagine Dad . . .' Her voice trailed away.

'I don't want to imagine it but, believe me, that's all that men think about.' Rosie was firm.

'I'd say they're just talking.' Helen was hopeful. 'What do you think, Anthony?'

Anthony as usual had heard nothing because he had his earphones in and was listening to music on his iPod. He knew he was being spoken to from their faces.

'Fine, it's all just fine with me,' he said agreeably.

The sisters exchanged weary glances.

Josie found to her surprise that her husband Harry was already at home. No jobs tonight, he said, a big reception where he was going to play had been cancelled.

'It's the downturn,' Harry said as he poured out two glasses of a very rough red wine. 'It's all due to the economy. There's no money for big receptions any more and, if there is, they don't have enough to pay a band.'

'Isn't it a bit early to be getting into the wine?' Josie asked mildly.

'It is – and it isn't. I don't have any gigs for the next three weeks so we'll be living on your earnings. That won't amount to many treats. Let's enjoy this.'

'I'm sure it's not as bad as all that,' Josie said.

'It is and worse,' said Harry. 'I met Liam Nolan on the way home, he got his cards today. Mash's business has gone belly up.'

'Liam's lost his job?' Josie was shocked.

'Yeah, he's probably in the process of telling Dee now. That's not going to go down well.'

'It's certainly not,' Josie agreed.

'Still, haven't they a great rake of children,

two girls and a boy, all grown up? They'll bail him out all right, won't they?'

'I wouldn't bet money on that . . .' Josie didn't think that Rosie, Anthony and Helen contributed much to the Nolan household.

'Well, they'd hardly be living there and paying nothing,' Harry said, savouring the terrible wine.

Things were very simple in Harry's life.

In a dark bar, Mash Macken was trying to do a deal with the owner who was busy polishing glasses.

'I'm having a few lads in here tonight,' he began. 'I have to give them a bit of bad news. I wonder, could we have something to eat, like maybe sausages and French bread and a bit of cheese?'

'Are you laying them off?' The man behind the bar had seen it all and knew it all.

'Yes, that's the situation,' Mash agreed gloomily.

'I'd say you'd need to push the boat out further than a few sandwiches,' the man said, still polishing the glasses. 'If it were me I'd think in terms of a few large brandies.'

'I've paid all their stamps, they'll get benefit.'

'Yeah, that's going to be something to look forward to,' said the barman.

Mash wondered had the fellow always been like this or was it just working in a bar that made him this way?

Dee had been tired already but now she felt totally exhausted. She sat on the bed and stretched out her legs.

Liam pulled his chair up beside her. He stroked her hair.

'Poor Dee,' he said. 'I wanted a better life for you, I really did.'

'Don't I have a great life?' she managed.

'But this . . . what will we do?'

'Will there be no one else hiring?' she asked, though she knew the answer. Mash had been living on borrowed time as it was.

'Not a whisper. I could try getting little cards printed like you have and set up as "Liam Nolan Electrical Repairs".' He smiled for a moment thinking about it, then his face changed. 'Along with a thousand others,' he added lamely.

'Whatever happens, Liam, we're not going to get down. We're not going to get into some black hole of depression over it. Do you hear me?'

'I hear you, but you *have* your job, Dee . . .' He looked beaten and sad.

'But that's all it is – a job. Yours is a career, a profession, a trade. Don't give up on us now, Liam, I beg you. I love you so much, I couldn't bear to see you all down.'

'I love you too.' He stroked her hand.

'Well then, aren't we luckier than a lot of people.' She had convinced herself by this stage, and her energy was coming back. 'Come on, Liam, let's go downstairs now and tell the children about it all.'

Dee got off the bed and looked at herself in the mirror. She ran a brush through her hair and put on a little lipstick. 'Here, smarten yourself up a bit, Liam. Don't let them see you defeated.'

'I *am* defeated, Dee.'

'Only if you let yourself be,' she said.

'Do you think we should leave telling them tonight? Maybe I'll get something else. No point in worrying them and upsetting them,' Liam said.

'We're a family – they must know. They are going to help us get through this.'

'But *gradually*, not in one big announcement. You know, I don't want to go down and say that I've lost my job, show them I can't keep a roof over their heads. I don't want to say it yet, Dee, not until we've looked at everything. Why involve them at this stage?'

'We can't protect them from this, Liam, it's too big. It's going to affect all of us. And they are all grown-ups now, they're in their twenties. They're not babies and we can't treat them like infants. They can all contribute to the running of the house. We're not driving them away, after all. Although if they did move out, we could maybe rent out their rooms . . . You and I had our own homes at their age . . .'

They went downstairs.

Nobody looked up.

Rosie still scanned her face in the mirror, Anthony smiled to himself as he sought and found further musical excitement on his iPod. Helen still worked on her plans for the school trip. She had almost assembled now the sheet of paper that she would show to the school principal as her final plan.

Nobody had opened the bag of shopping that Dee had bought so carefully in the supermarket, hunting down bargains all over the store. The bag stood where it had been left, leaning against the table. The question of supper had not been considered by anyone, any more than the matter of clearing up after lunch. The bundle of clean, dry clothes stood by the washing machine as it had done at four this morning.

Dee felt a huge tiredness across her shoulders, the kind of tiredness that might never go away. How had it got to this? Was she responsible for their selfishness? Was it her fault they contributed nothing at all to the running of the house? Was it Liam's fault?

'Here we all are,' Liam said to his three grown-up children. 'A full house, that's what I like to see . . .'

Anthony raised his eyes from the tiny screen he was watching. 'Great!' he said enthusiastically and went straight back to the screen.

Rosie put on more lip salve and made further faces at her own reflection.

Only Helen showed any interest. She looked at the faces of her parents, from one to the other and back.

'There's nothing wrong is there, Mam? Dad?'

'Well, nothing we can't work out together,' Liam said.

'Bad times for all of us. Your dad and I were just talking about it. Mash Macken's business has gone under. We thought he was safe but it turns out none of our jobs are safe.'

'Oh, isn't that *terrible!*' Helen said.

'What's terrible?' Rosie asked.

Dee said nothing.

'Dad and Mam were saying that things are bad for Mash Macken, no jobs are safe,' Helen explained.

'Tell me about it, there's no work out there,' Anthony agreed.

'But it may not be as bad as it looks,' Liam said soothingly.

'Or of course it could be even worse than it looks.' Dee was clipped.

'Why, Mam? Why do you always see the bad side of things?' Rosie had a particular sort of whine that must have contributed greatly to the serious marital difficulties that she and Ronan were going through.

Something had got through to Anthony. He had not put his earphones on again, and was looking from one face to another to catch up.

'Will we have enough money?' he asked simply.

Dee looked at him in wonder. He had always been an easy child to rear, dreamy, in a world of his own. He was always willing to help, if reminded half a dozen times. He always hoped that there would soon be recognition of his musical talents, and fame and world success would follow. Then he could have a big comfortable house for his parents, a home by the sea. But he still looked at his father's impending unemployment from his own point of view.

'Would we have enough money?' was all he wanted to know. Nothing about how he could go out and earn some money – nothing from any one of the three of them about that.

'Did he pay your stamps, Da?' Rosie enquired.

'Yes, he did, and if—'

'Ah well, you'll be fine then.' For Rosie it was a problem solved.

'You get an income and no need to go out to work? Won't that be great altogether, Da? I'd love that on a Monday morning,' Helen said.

Dee looked at her. At least she was the only one of them who did have a proper job. But she had never contributed a cent to the house where she lived. The thought had never crossed her mind. When Dee had mentioned it to Liam, he had always said, *nonsense, it was her home*.

But Dee felt she must explain unemployment benefit more fully.

'Your father paid in to his stamps, just like Mash Macken did. So he'll get around half his week's wages, his entitlement, do you understand? He is entitled to that money.'

'Keep your shirt on, Mam,' Rosie said.

'There's no problem then.' Anthony loved things to be sorted.

'Don't always be bringing Dad down,' Helen pleaded.

Dee snapped. 'You are three great selfish lumps! Look at yourselves, just sitting there, letting me wait on you hand and foot. It's time you lot woke up – there are going to be some changes around here. Yes, I thought that might shock you. But if you're going to carry on living here – *if* you're going to keep on living here – you're going to have to contribute to the household just as much as you would if you were living anywhere else.'

The uproar was instant. Rosie and Helen immediately started protesting at the tops of their voices – *imagine* Mam's bad timing, trying to break up the family at this stage. When Dad had got bad news about being laid off! Had she no understanding at all? Anthony simply stared at her in shock. Liam immediately tried to pat everyone down.

'Nonsense, Dee, of course they live here. This is their home and they're as welcome as the flowers in May and always will be. Of course they'll all help out. You're just tired. Now, come on everyone, give your mother a hand.

You clear the table and I'll unpack the shopping. Isn't that right, Dee? You've had a bit of a shock, we all have. That's all it is – we'll get through this, we'll all pull together.'

'No, Liam, no, it's not good enough. We'll manage fine but only if we make some changes . . .' She tried to speak in a clear and reasonable tone. 'I'm not trying to throw you out, of course I'm not. But I'm going to have to try to get a bit more work to tide us over while Dad looks for another job. We need you three to contribute to the household budget as well. You need to think about how you can do that.

'You can start by feeding yourselves. Don't count on me to put meals on the table for you. If I'm working even more hours, I can't be cooking for you as well. And you'll have to look after your own washing and ironing – you all know how the washing machine works. Anthony, it's time you looked for a job yourself. Rosie, Helen, you need to think about how much you can afford to pay for your room . . .'

Then all the shock, all the shouting began again. Rosie had sunk all her money into the house she no longer shared with Ronan. Helen had poured everything into the school trip she was organising. Anthony pointed out that the job market was every bit as bad for his generation as for Dad's. They resented Dee, it was clear, they said she wasn't being supportive, they turned to Liam. And Liam, once again, tried to soothe everything down.

Dee sighed. They lived rent-free in this house and ate the food she put in front of them and let her iron their clothes. How could she make them see how unfair it was?

As the noise subsided, Dee picked up the bag of shopping. Mechanically she unpacked all the contents, stacking the yoghurts in the fridge, moving the half-carton of low-fat spread to the front and putting the newer ones behind.

Milk. Someone had always finished the milk or left the carton out so that it went sour.

Dee had bought the smaller and more expensive cartons. It was better value to buy the big two-litre cartons but not if they were going to waste it . . .

Dee was so familiar with this routine that it only took a few minutes. She left the lamb on a wooden board at the kitchen sink. Chop, chop, she soon had the big saucepan full of meat and vegetables. Then she added a stock cube and some water, and soon it was bubbling away. Food for five adult people. Shopped for by Dee, unpacked by Dee, paid for with the money Dee earned cleaning office buildings, and later to be served by Dee.

She moved seamlessly to the ironing with a handful of those wire hangers you get at the cleaners. First she did Liam's shirts. Four of them. She was particularly careful about the collars. Then she folded the girls' blouses, dresses and underwear neatly and put them all clean but un-ironed into one laundry basket, and all Anthony's things into another. It was a small thing, and it would be followed by a series of other small things. But it would work.

She frowned. There were going to be changes, whether they liked it or not. She would have to make her own plans.

Rosie had gone back to catch the late afternoon and early evening crowds in the shopping mall and direct them towards a complimentary make-up and hopefully to buy a lot of cosmetics. Anthony was still absorbed by his machine, Helen in her pile of pictures and timetables. Liam was reading the Situations Vacant column in the evening paper.

None of them had any idea how much things were going to change.

Chapter Three

Very early next morning Josie wondered whether to mention the subject of Liam. She decided she would wait and judge the mood.

Dee seemed thoughtful as they drove through the sleeping city.

'Everything all right at home?' Josie asked gently.

'Grand, and yourself?'

'Oh, Harry had a gig cancelled. He was very annoyed, and took to real rot-gut wine to get himself over it.'

'Liam got his cards too,' Dee said quietly.

'He what? His job's gone?' Josie knew already – because Harry had talked to Liam. What she didn't know was how Dee remained so calm.

'Yes, it's going to mean a big change for all of us,' Dee said carefully.

Josie couldn't understand Dee's reaction at all. 'You're taking it very well, I'll say that much for you,' she said in the end.

'What other way is there to take it? And talking about taking things, could you and Harry use some breakfast cereal, and some eggs and maybe a couple of packs of biscuits?'

'The ones you bought yesterday at the super-market?' This was getting odder by the moment, thought Josie.

'Yes indeed,' Dee said.

'Where are they?' Josie asked.

'In that green bag in the back of the van. Oh, and there's a nice iced cherry log in there too.'

'Dee, why are you doing this?'

'Well, I'm not going to *sell* them to you, am I? I'm giving them to you.'

'You paid the money you earned cleaning floors for that food and now you're giving it away?'

'It's not needed any more,' Dee said simply.

'But Dee, don't you need it more than ever now? Please be reasonable.'

'I'm being very reasonable, believe me. And, Josie, either take the food – or don't take it – but can we not talk about it again today?'

Dee settled back in her seat and Josie drove on in a very rare and unusual silence until they got to work.

Dee's strange mood continued all day. It was as if she had been given her happy pills. Nothing annoyed her, not the messy Sonia who had left some table napkins smeared with lipstick and food, with a note saying, *Darlings, the laundry won't do these, can you work some stain magic on them? Please . . .*

She didn't get annoyed by the thoughtless young men in their new shining offices who had flung paper cups that still contained coffee into waste-paper baskets so that they created a mush and a mess. Dee was almost serene.

Josie couldn't understand it at all. When the day finally ended for them, Josie said that she was just dying for that sandwich. She had been thinking about it for the last two hours. Maybe a tuna melt? Or a chilli chicken wrap?

But no. Dee-of-the-surprises had yet one more. She wasn't going to join Josie for a sandwich: she was going to go straight home. No, thank you, she didn't want a lift. She would take a bus part of the way and walk the rest.

'Did I do something to annoy you?' Josie asked, because she was totally confused.

'Aw, Josie, will you stop it, of course you didn't.'

'But Dee, we *always* have a bit of lunch . . .'

'You sound seven years of age, Jo!' Dee laughed at her and gave her a hug. 'Why don't you go home yourself – and don't forget what I left you in the green bag in the back of the van.'

'There's no sweet chilli chicken in it, is there?' Josie wanted to know.

'See you tomorrow.'

Dee swung off towards the bus stop leaving Josie not knowing what to do next. She had been planning that sandwich and a big frothy coffee for half the morning, but now she wondered would it be more sensible to go straight home with Dee's green bag? But Dee had been so odd today there could be *anything* in that bag . . .

Anthony was sitting at the table at home in number sixteen.

'How are you, Ma?' He greeted her with a big grin. He had such an eager smile. She forced herself not to ask him if he had eaten any lunch.

'All well with you, Anthony?'

'Fine, Ma. What are you making?'

She knew what he meant – he wanted to know what was for supper – but she pretended not to.

Instead she said, 'What am I making? Let me see. Let's say eight hours a day, five days a week on the minimum wage, what does that come to? You do the sums.'

He looked up at her, startled. 'I wasn't trying

to pry, Ma, honestly . . . I didn't mean that, I only meant what's for . . .' His voice trailed away.

'No, that's fine, love. I thought you were worried, like we all are, about Dad losing his job and whether we would manage. I was wondering whether you'd had any luck yet trying to get a job, or a girlfriend who might interest you more than your music. I was thinking that most men your age go out and work for a living and leave the nest. Instead of expecting their mums and dads to provide everything for them all of the time . . .'

'But it's all right, isn't it? Dad will get a proper amount every week, won't he? I mean, he said it wasn't anything to worry about,' Anthony replied, bewildered.

'Is that what Dad said?' Dee sounded surprised. 'That's not what I heard. I heard him say we all had to pull together and I'm just asking how you plan to help out. Right, so now, what are your plans for the evening?'

'Plans?'

'Yes, I was wondering what you were going to do?' Dee said.

'Well, nothing in particular, just . . . just the usual, Ma.'

'Right, love, and where will you do this *usual*?'

'Well, here. I mean, here at the table, isn't that all right?'

'Not tonight, love. Your dad and I need the table to work out some figures. We need some space to spread things out.'

'But you have a table in your bedroom.'

'No, that's a little fancy table for ornaments and hairbrushes,' Dee explained patiently.

'You don't have any of those on it, Ma.'

'No, but I might some day! Anyway about tonight? You can work in your own room, can't you?'

'It's a bit small and cramped, Ma.'

'I know, Anthony, I know. Small and cramped. This is what happens,' Dee said. She sounded sympathetic.

Anthony felt that all this was somehow unfamiliar. 'Yes, well, I suppose it is. What time's supper?' he asked.

'Supper?' Dee looked surprised that he had asked.

'Like, what time are we eating?' Anthony explained.

'Oh, whenever you like, of course. Your dad and I will be having a lamb chop around six-thirty before we get on with our paperwork.'

'Lamb chops, that will be grand.' Anthony's face lit up.

This was harder than Dee believed possible. It had to be Anthony, of course, the gentlest of them. Maybe Liam's way was right. After all, it *was* their home, and Anthony had a right to expect his supper. But no, she couldn't break her resolution now.

'Oh, I was only making supper for your dad and myself. I was thinking that, after our little talk, the rest of you would have your own plans.' She tried to look bright and pleasant about it all.

'So there's no supper, is that it?' he said glumly.

'Nonsense, love, aren't the chip shops full of food – or a Chinese takeaway, maybe?'

'Or we might make something here?' Anthony wanted to keep some hold on normality.

'Well, sure, but don't take those two rashers and the eggs, they're for your father's breakfast, and you'll make sure not to use up all the milk . . .'

'No, Mam.'

'Right, I'm off upstairs to have a bit of a rest. I'll see you later on.'

'Right, Mam.'

His eyes followed her as she left the room.

Normally she would have made him tea, given him a slice of apple tart and tried to draw him out. Mam always wanted to know what Anthony was thinking. He was mainly thinking about music, which was hard to explain sometimes. But today she was totally different. As if he weren't all that important or something. Or as if Mam had her mind outside the house, away from the family. But that couldn't be. Surely?

Anthony went to the fridge to get himself something to eat. It was almost empty. On one plate were two lamb chops, on another two bacon rashers and two eggs. There had been plenty of food in it yesterday.

Something very strange indeed was happening here.

In the shopping mall Rosie had managed to draw several passers-by to the cosmetic counter. She had a good manner with the customers.

'Excuse me, is that a new jacket? It's *beautiful*.' Then she would offer the lady her little business card. 'I'm from this company and we are offering complimentary make-up at our counter. Perhaps with this jacket you might consider a more vibrant lipstick? Anyway, do come in and see what we have. No obligation to buy . . .'

Bella, who ran the counter, watched her admiringly. She was impressed. This girl, Rosie, had style. She would offer her a six-week training course with the company. She had exactly the pert, lively interest in strangers that would make her a good saleswoman. And she was tough too. She was quick to work out her percentage of everything the customers bought. Rosie was always faster than the calculator. She would enjoy six weeks in London.

Helen had been called to the principal's office.

'This must stop *now*, Miss Nolan, this moment. There will be no tour of Paris for pupils from this school. Not this Easter, not any Easter.'

'But – they're so looking forward to it, it would break their hearts!'

'Which is why it should never have been suggested.'

'But it's all planned, they know all the places they are going to visit . . .'

'Places they are *not* going to visit.'

'But it's all arranged!'

'Then you must un-arrange it, Miss Nolan, today. There is no insurance in the world that would cover this. You would need four teachers, not one, and even then it's not possible. It's most irresponsible of you to promise the pupils something that can't be delivered. I will hear from you before the end of school today that it has all been dismantled.'

Liam had found the day very long. He had got the little cards printed and then he had gone as arranged to meet Mash Macken and the other lads. Last night in the bar had been silent and awkward. Mash was doing his best to tell them that he would do anything to save the business, that he *had* done everything in fact: invested his own money and mortgaged his house. He was going to Australia penniless. He wanted them to come to the premises and take what would be useful.

Liam hated going there. So many mornings had begun with mugs of tea and a laugh about the day ahead. The others felt the same. And they knew there was no future for a skilled carpenter, joiner or plumber. Not the way the market was at the moment. They all wanted to be away from it but Mash insisted they take anything and everything.

'I've nowhere to store things, Mash,' Liam had said in desperation. 'I know that's a lovely bit of wood, but honestly, I've nowhere to put it. The house is full, with three big children there as well as Dee and myself . . .'

'Will they help to support you, the children?' Mash was aching for some kind of hope in all this gloomy business.

Liam paused for a moment. Mash Macken wanted to hear some good news for someone before he took a flight to the other side of the world. Liam gave it to him.

'Oh God, Mash, they're the finest family you could wish for. They'll be a great support, the three of them.'

He saw Mash relax a little and he thought for the first time how good it would be if this was really true. If he really did have a son and two daughters who understood how hard it was for their parents to keep supporting them. And because he was Liam he immediately felt guilty about that thought.

Chapter Four

Liam arrived home at around the same time as his daughter Helen.

Helen seemed to have totally forgotten Liam's woes as she began to list her own before she was even in the door.

'Such a narrow-minded man, such a *bad* person to be in charge of a school!' she said. 'How did someone like that get to be principal? And they wonder why children leave school half educated!' She came in and flung herself down at the kitchen table.

'There's no supper,' Anthony said.

'Oh, for God's sake, Anthony, think about something else, not always about food. I'll eat whatever's going, not that I ever want to eat again. Wait until I tell you what's happened! Mam – are you listening?'

'No, Helen,' her mother said.

Helen was shocked. 'But Mam, why aren't you? The most awful thing has happened at work . . . you have no idea.'

Dee shook her head to deny this. 'Oh, I do

have an idea, Helen. I had an awful day at work too, and your dad had an awful day going up to Mash Macken's and having no work – so honestly, we do understand.'

Helen felt stopped in her tracks. 'Yes, well, I know it's awful, Mam, I've always said—'

'What have you always said?'

Her mother was being perfectly polite, but there was something different about the way she spoke, as if she were an outsider, a friend of the family, yes, but not *Mam*.

'I always say . . . that you work very hard, Mam, put in terrible hours and all . . .'

'Yes, yes, and who do you say that *to*, exactly, Helen?'

'Well, anyone really.'

'Oh good, it's just that you never said it to me, so it comes as a surprise.'

'Mam, they've cancelled my school outing, they won't let me take the children to Paris.' Tears weren't far away.

'That's very disappointing for you all right. Liam – how was *your* day?'

'Terrible, we couldn't wait to be out of Mash Macken's place and he didn't want us to go. It was desperate.'

'Well, love, that's the very worst bit over. All

you have to do now is sign on and look around for a bit of work here and there.'

Helen noticed that her mother was handing a mug of tea to Liam but there wasn't one for anyone else.

'Well, anyway, that's it,' Helen said. 'The principal says the trip's off, that the insurance won't cover it. That there would need to be four teachers with the group if we were going and that the parents would think it too risky anyway. The children are so upset – and I've already paid the deposit to the travel agent . . .' Her voice trailed away.

Nobody was listening. Her mother and father were talking to each other. Helen looked hopefully at Anthony.

'I don't know if she means no supper just today or for every day,' he said, worried. 'I didn't like the look on her face. Did we *do* anything to annoy her?'

'Of course we didn't!' Helen snapped and then she paused. Why was Mam behaving like this, at the very time that Dad needed a peaceful place to live? Mam could be really selfish at times. She wasn't even listening to Helen's problems, let alone saying anything sympathetic.

*

Ronan paused outside the door. He was never sure what kind of welcome he would get these days – Rosie had probably told them all terrible tales about him. But he had to see her, he had to try and talk to her.

Dee answered the door to him.

'Ah, Ronan,' she said as if he were an elderly neighbour, or someone to be greeted with courtesy if not enthusiasm.

'Mrs Nolan, Dee, could I have a word with Rosie, do you think?'

'She's not home yet, Ronan, but come in and sit down to wait for her.'

'She might not want to see me.' He looked and sounded about twelve years of age.

'Well then, you will obviously take your troubles out of the house . . .'

'Sorry?' Ronan said, confused.

'I'm sure you *are* sorry and I'm sure Rosie is. But you will discuss it out of our home. It's not our battle after all.' Dee sounded polite but firm.

Ronan remembered many battles fought between him and Rosie at this very table with the family sitting silently, looking stricken by it all. Perhaps he and Rosie *had* been a bit noisy here once or twice. But there was something different about Mrs Nolan this evening. Ronan wished he knew what it was.

He decided to concentrate on Liam. 'How's work, Mr Nolan?' he asked cheerfully.

Liam was beginning to find a vague answer, but Dee interrupted.

'It isn't any more. Liam's been let go, we were just talking about how to manage. How we were *all* going to have to manage.'

'Oh yes, yes, of course,' Ronan said. 'Yes, I imagine everyone has to do something.' He looked around him wildly. Judging from their faces, this seemed quite far from either Helen's or Anthony's thoughts.

Just then Rosie came in and flung her very high-heeled shoes across the room.

'You'll never guess what's happened,' she said and then without waiting for a response, 'I'm going to London! They're sending me on a course. It's going to be fantastic. Six whole weeks! I'll get to stay in a swanky hotel and eat in all the restaurants and go to all the clubs. I might not come back at all – it's going to be great.' She sat rubbing her feet. 'I'll need some more shoes. They make me wear these up and down the mall: it's exhausting. You want to see the mall sometime, Mam, and imagine me walking a hundred miles a day in those heels!'

'I do know the mall, I was there this morning getting a job, actually,' Dee said.

They all looked up in surprise.

'I've got six hours shelf-stacking in the supermarket.' Dee looked around, pleased.

Liam was concerned. 'You're taking on too much, love,' he said.

Anthony was amazed. 'How would you know what to put where, Mam?' he asked.

Helen was thoughtless. 'I'll probably be there beside you, Mam, if the travel agency won't let me have the deposit back. I'll have to take any old job I can find.'

Rosie was about to speak when she noticed Ronan for the first time. 'Oh, *you* are here,' she said with no sign of any pleasure.

'Yes. I thought we should talk before you head off for London . . .' he began.

'We've talked all the talk there is, Ronan, and if you think—' Her voice was raised dangerously.

'Not here, Rosie.' He looked over at Dee and Liam. 'This isn't their battle but it *is* their home. We can talk somewhere else . . .'

'If you think for one moment that I am going back to that house where I was so unhappy—'

Ronan spoke in a slow measured voice.

'A café, please, Rosie,' he said – and his words had the right effect.

She calmed down. 'Right,' she said after a pause. 'I'll get my shoes.'

They were gone and the rest of the family seemed to give a sigh of relief that they had been spared yet another of those '*You said* and *you said* and *you said*' conversations that led nowhere – except to Rosie bursting into tears and Ronan flouncing out the door.

'That's a relief. I wonder how Ronan thought of that,' Anthony said.

'I wonder,' Dee agreed.

'Mam just said it to him,' Helen said. She was annoyed with Mam for not listening but fair was fair.

'By the way, Helen, you may find it harder to get a job shelf-stacking than you think. There were sixty people there today, after four places.'

'Sure, Mam.' Helen's voice was low.

But Dee seemed bright.

'So, anyway, I won't keep you two. Dad and I have to work here at the table so we'll let you go now. Is that all right?'

'Go where?' Helen asked.

'Well, I don't know really, that's up to you. Out maybe? You might want to think about getting yourselves some supper. Or up to your rooms? You both have a room.'

'But it's a bedroom!' Helen said.

'It's a *room*,' Mam countered.

'Sure.' Helen knew there was no chance here of anyone hearing her story and sympathising over the bad news the day had brought her. 'But I think I'll go down to Maud and Marco's. At least there'll be some food and a bit of conversation there. And if Rosie is going to be banging on about her trip to London, I might ask them if I can stay there for a few days.'

Anthony finally realised that he too was being edged out. He gathered up his iPod, his notebooks and his earphones into the leather bag he carried. He looked back from the stairs with suspicion as he saw his mother spread out papers and accounts books on the table.

Dee and Liam studied the figures on the sheets of paper.

'It's no use,' Liam said in the end. 'Even if I *did* get a good bit of private work, it would never add up.'

'What should we give up?' Dee asked.

'I won't go for a pint,' Liam offered.

'That's nothing,' Dee said. 'You've never been a big drinker. Anyway, you need to talk to people in pubs to find out where there's any work.'

'But what else?' His face was drawn and worried.

'If the children can't see their way to paying us some rent, we might have to let a room,' Dee said eventually.

'We can't, Dee, and even if Rosie does go back to that fellow, Helen and Anthony have to have a room each.'

'But not necessarily here in this house,' Dee said.

'It's their home.' Liam wouldn't change his mind on this.

Dee tried a different route.

'Listen, Rosie's going away anyway for six weeks. Helen's going to stay with Maud, she's always going on about how welcoming they are there. She can stay there while Rosie's away and we could get some rent from the front room.'

'But wouldn't we have some stranger on top of us?' Liam was anxious.

'We could give them a kettle and a hotplate.' Dee was ready.

'You've thought it all through,' Liam said, alarmed.

'No I haven't, I was just thinking of our Taormina fund,' Dee said.

This year they would be twenty-five years married. They had been saving for a holiday in Sicily, in the same resort where they had spent their honeymoon, and every year had promised to go back. None of the money they had put in the china jug had been taken out. But there was hardly enough for a deposit, let alone a holiday.

'I'd love to go back,' Liam said.

'Then we will,' Dee said.

They got out more paper and did more sums. How much could they charge a lodger? They knew what people paid for a room round here. It would be a great help filling up the china jug for the holiday in Sicily.

'It will be great,' Dee pronounced. She sounded much more confident than she was. There would be many battles ahead, she knew.

The first battle was with Rosie. She stormed in the door just as they were eating their lamb chops.

'That smells nice,' she said, 'but I'll only have them if you cut off the fat, I hate even looking at it. Wait until I tell you what his new plan is. To sell the house. *Sell? Now?* Nobody is buying houses now. Does Ronan live in the real world,

I ask you? If you're doing tomatoes, I'd like them lightly grilled, not swimming in fat.'

Dee looked at her daughter, beautiful, well groomed, her shiny blonde hair expertly cut – one of the perks of the job. Her face was without concern or care for anyone except herself. Dee wondered how her daughter had become so spoiled.

'Did I tell you I was starting work in the mall next week, Rosie?'

'Yes, I think you did, Mam. Where are the others? Why aren't they here?'

'Anthony went to get a pizza, I think.'

'Is he bringing it back?'

'No, I think he's eating it there. And Helen has gone to see her friend, Maud. She's thinking of staying there with Maud and Marco while you're away in London.'

'She never is. Why?'

'To give us a room to let.'

'But that's *my* room too!' Rosie cried.

She looked to her father for confirmation. But for once he didn't run to her defence.

'You won't be using it, Rosie. You'll be in a hotel in London. Surely you'd like your mother and myself to try and make something out of an empty room?'

'But it's not an empty room. It's our home,' Rosie said.

Isn't she a little minx, Dee thought to herself. Using the very phrase her father always used. Swiftly she changed the subject.

'I'll be able to see you in the mall in the afternoons. I'm going to be doing afternoon shelf-stacking. You know, goods they have run out of in the morning – and you stand near the door of the supermarket, don't you?'

'Mam, if you even approach me when I'm doing my work, I'll . . . well, I don't know what I'll do . . . You're going to stack shelves, right?'

'Right.'

'In a yellow nylon coat? Right?'

'I think so, possibly, yes.'

'That's what they wear,' said Rosie. 'I see them from time to time, when they come out for a smoke. Mam, you wouldn't talk to me, would you?'

Something happened to Dee at that moment. Her voice became very cold.

'No, Rosie, I wouldn't. Believe me, I wouldn't go near you, approach you, or say hello to my own daughter. It would be out of the question.'

'Rosie doesn't mean it like that, Dee,' Liam, the peacemaker, began.

'No, but I do. I wouldn't cross the mall to talk

to someone like Rosie.' There was something about the way she said it that made Rosie uneasy.

'Listen, Mam, I'm a bit upset, you know, Ronan being such a clown and everything. Let's just have supper and forget it.'

'Your father and I have just had our supper. You must have yours wherever you please. And if you are having it in your room, then would you think about putting your clothes into storage? We will need that room from Monday, the day after you leave.'

Rosie began to speak but her mother would have none of it.

'And no, Rosie, I will *not* forget it. I've had a long day cleaning office floors, washing stains off table napkins, cleaning bathrooms and vacuuming long halls. I'm pleased that I got myself a few more hours stacking shelves. I never wondered before why I did it for years and still do it and face years more ahead doing it. But tonight I wonder. And since I get up at four in the morning, I think I'll go to bed now where I can wonder more about it . . .'

'Aw, Mam, don't take it like that!' Rosie called to her mother, who was already halfway up the stairs. There was no reply.

Rosie looked at her father.

'I'm with your mother on this one,' he said simply.

'If you had wanted rent for the room, you should have asked,' Rosie said. 'We can't all be inspired or something.'

'Goodnight.'

Rosie had never seen her father's face so closed, so unloving.

This had been some day. They must have a crisis meeting soon. Things were far from normal round here.

Chapter Five

They would have to have a council of war. Rosie knew that for certain. She went to her room and called Helen at Maud and Marco's place.

'We're just sitting down to supper,' Helen complained.

'Lucky old you, there's nothing to eat here.'

'I know, Mam's taken a real sort of turn over something. She wouldn't even listen when I tried to tell her . . .'

Rosie decided she must interrupt or else she would be talking about Helen's school trip for the rest of the night.

'You're right, she *has* taken a turn. But, wait for it, Dad says he's with her on this. He just walked out of the room, and wouldn't discuss it.'

'Discuss what?'

'They're letting our room.'

'She only says that – she doesn't mean it.' Helen sounded stunned.

'She does mean it. I'll be gone to London and

she says you prefer to live with Maud and Marco . . . one empty room. Solution – let it to a lodger.'

'Yes, maybe, but not forever, that wouldn't be fair.'

'Fair? Who wouldn't it be fair on?' Rosie asked.

'Us!' Helen said. 'It's our home.'

'I don't think that one's going to work much longer,' Rosie said.

'Well, it mightn't work for *you*. But then *you* have a home to go to and a husband who keeps coming around to ask you to come back. I have nowhere, nothing except a huge debt to a travel agency. I can't afford anywhere to live.'

'You're twenty-two years old, and you have a teacher's salary. Other teachers who are not from Dublin have places to live.'

'Yes, but they don't have big unfair debts to travel agencies.'

'You only got that debt today.'

'So what? I still have to pay it.'

'We have to have a meeting, Helen.'

'No we don't, I have to go and have my supper. Mam and Dad more or less pushed me out of St Jarlath's Crescent. I don't want to be pushed out of here as well.'

'I'll round up Anthony and we'll meet tomorrow.'

'Where? At home?'

'Don't be stupid, Helen.'

'Well, where then?'

'I'll think. I'll text you,' Rosie said.

'Everything OK?' Helen's friend Maud asked as she served the pasta.

'Don't ask what's all right and what's not, let's just eat!' said Marco, smiling.

Oh, wouldn't life be great if everyone was as easy-going as Marco and Maud, thought Helen. Perhaps it *was* unfair to expect Mam to put food on the table all that time, but as Dad said, it *was* their home.

And if the finger should be pointed, why was it at her? Helen was the only one of them earning a proper living. Anthony had never worked. Never. Rosie had gone and got married – that lasted ten minutes and then she was back hustling for victims in a shopping mall. At least Helen had studied, done her exams, trained as a teacher. They should be *pleased* with her, rather than suggesting she leave her room free. Last year at her graduation they had said they were so proud of her. Why weren't they still proud? Why did they ask her to go away so that they could let her room? It was a mystery.

'Stop frowning, Helen, you'll get dreadful lines in your face and Rosie will drag you in to get them removed,' Maud teased her.

'Helen will never have dreadful lines on her face. Stop frightening her!' Marco said. 'She will be lucky like you were, Maud, and meet a marvellous Italian love . . .' Marco put his arm around Maud's neck. 'She too will find a magical Italian for herself, just like you did!'

'Oh, Marco!' Maud pretended to be shocked. 'You believe that a man is the solution for everything. You are ridiculous!'

Ronan said that he would drive Rosie to the airport.

'I'm going for six weeks to London. I am a free person, leading a free life,' she insisted.

'I know that, Rosie. I am saving your bus fare, that's all.'

'My company will pay for that.' She sounded more confident than she felt.

'Let me save them the fare instead,' he offered, rattling the car keys.

'Oh no, I'd get nothing but how great every thing was until I walked out. I don't want one word about how good it was . . . It was hellish, that's what it was.'

'I don't remember it as all bad,' he said.

61

'You don't because you were out the whole time and I was cleaning the place and cooking for you and ironing. My God, the ironing of a clean shirt every day . . .'

'I could do the ironing,' Ronan said.

'You could, you always could have, but did you? You never did. Never, not once.'

'I would now.'

'No, you'd do it for two days. Then you'd be off out again.'

'Rosie, I went out to work, for you and for me. You knew that's what I did. I never said I'd stay at home all day and play house.'

'But you were *never* at home.'

'I had to visit customers, I told you that you could come with me.'

'Stand in pubs and be pawed by drunks? No thank you.'

'But that's my job, selling packets of snacks to pubs. Pubs – that's where I work, Rosie. Be fair!'

'Fair? I was *very* fair. You should know what *some* women would do, then you'd say I was fair. I walked away, said we'd made a mistake, that it wasn't working. What's unfair about that? It was the truth. We were fighting all the time.'

'But we *must* have loved each other, to get married?' Ronan was puzzled.

Rosie felt weary. 'Listen, when I get back from London we *will* talk again, Ronan. Really we will. That's if I have a place to lay my head. My mother is starting to turn my home into a guest house and is going to boot us all out.'

'Why is that?' Ronan liked his mother-in-law: it didn't seem in her character to do such a thing.

'I don't know, money, I think.'

'Well, why don't you all pay her something?'

'It's our *home*, Ronan. You don't pay at home.'

'I did when I lived at home,' Ronan said.

'That's because your family are half mad,' Rosie said, but she felt uneasy.

Dee and Josie looked forward to going to see their client, Miss Mason.

Miss Mason told them that it was her sixty-fourth birthday. They both pretended to be amazed. In fact they had thought she was around eighty. Miss Mason looked so frail and didn't go out to work. How could she be so young?

They made a fuss of her, slipped out and got a small cake and sang 'Happy Birthday' with their mugs of tea.

She clapped her hands and said it was all marvellous. She said that her niece Lily was coming to see her around teatime, so Josie and Dee prepared a little tea tray for the occasion.

Lily lived in the country but apparently she was changing her plans. She was going to come and live in Dublin and she would be looking for somewhere to live. Dee and Josie had met Lily a few times. She was a tall, pale girl in a long cardigan, very fond of her aunt and always bringing her some well-chosen gift. A footstool, a magazine-rack for beside her chair, a really good reading light.

'I could offer her a room in my house for a few weeks until she finds her feet,' Dee suggested suddenly.

Josie's jaw fell open. 'But you don't have a free room. St Jarlath's Crescent – they're all three-bedroom houses, aren't they?' she said to Dee, puzzled.

'I do indeed have a room. Liam's painting it today. It's the girls' old room.'

'And where are the girls?' Josie was finding Dee very hard to follow these days.

'Rosie's going to London to do a sales course in cosmetics.'

'And Helen?'

'She's staying with a friend.'

'Well now, wouldn't that be great then?' Josie was pleased to see things working out well for Dee.

'So *is* there a room, Dee?' Miss Mason wondered.

'It would be simple, but she'd be very welcome.'

'She's a nurse, so she wouldn't have a fortune, but she'd pay the going rate. I'd love her to stay with you, Dee. She's a trusting girl and I feel like a mother to her. I don't want her here because she'd be looking after me, not having a life of her own.'

'We might be a bit dull for her.'

'No, I want her to be safe as well. She's been a home bird for too long.'

'She's your sister's child, right?'

'Yes, my sister Laura, that's right. Lucky Laura they called her.'

'Was she lucky?' Dee asked. Miss Mason never talked about her sister at all.

'She was. She got every single thing she ever wanted.' There was a big sigh and no more information.

Dee busied herself and finished up. Miss Mason was sitting in her chair, still looking right in front of her.

'I'll be off now, Miss Mason. I have put my

address on this note and my phone number. I'll be at home this afternoon if your niece would like to come and see if it suits her.'

'I'm sure she'll love it, Dee.' Her face was still sad.

As they got into Josie's van, Dee wondered what was the story in Miss Mason's family.

'No love between the sisters there,' Josie said.

'She's a nice girl, that Lily. I hope she'll like the place.'

Lily loved the place.

'What a beautiful room, all clean and shiny and with a window-box too! It's beautiful, Mrs Nolan.'

'I'm Dee and this is Liam. Do you really like it?'

'It's great – when can I move in? This week-end?'

'The smell of paint should have gone by then,' Liam said.

'Then I'll pay you a month in advance – is that all right?' Lily offered.

'Well, if you're sure, here's the house key,' Dee said.

After Lily left, Dee showed Liam the money. He couldn't believe it. They danced together around the kitchen. This was serious money. It meant they might make it through the difficult times. It might, it just *might* be all right.

Anthony came in and watched them for a while. Round and round they went. Then he sat down with his mobile to text his two sisters.

You asked me to tell you how things were going. Well, they couldn't be worse. There's been nothing to eat for three days, the house reeks of paint and turpentine and now they're dancing around the kitchen. Dancing as if there was music. They've gone completely mad.

Anthony

Chapter Six

Lily had settled in very well, *too* well, Anthony thought. It was a different world at home nowadays.

He texted his sisters regularly about it all, but he felt that they hadn't quite taken on board how serious it all was. And how very much life had altered – and not for the better.

Lily was a nurse at St Brigid's hospital; she was gone at seven-thirty in the morning and made her own supper when she came back home. There was no sitting around the kitchen table these evenings. Dad and Mam were always busy, looking at maps of Sicily, painting some old back shed or helping Lily in the thrift shop where she worked a few nights a week.

Some days Lily visited her aunt, the one that Mam knew up in the posh flats. She liked to prepare a little supper for the two of them, she said. It was hard to describe her. She had a nice face like a Madonna: she could be any age – twenty-five, thirty-five, forty-five. Impossible to say, really. She had straight fair hair, and she wore a long grey cardigan most of the time. She had her own shelf in the fridge with health foods and funny drinks made from beans or coconuts.

Mam said she was delighted with Lily. A nicer-mannered girl it would be hard to find, and even though she paid good rent she always played a part in the house. She slaved over the place at weekends. There she was now, out digging with Liam in the garden. She was even teaching them to play bridge. That was a *very* complicated game where you were meant to be telling your partner what you had in your hand but mainly you told them something baffling instead.

Helen and Rosie read these texts and were greatly confused by them.

Had Anthony gone mad? Mam and Dad playing bridge? Separate shelves in the fridge? It didn't bode well for their return.

Helen had offered to pay Maud and Marco for staying in their house but they said no, not at all. She was a friend, she was only going to be there a couple of days, she must stay like any friend. So she thought she must contribute something – maybe bring them food, but then that was ridiculous since they ran a restaurant themselves.

She meant to think of something else they would like, but she was so busy. There was school work and the threats from the travel agency and the worrying reports from Anthony at home. There wasn't a spare minute in the day until she would come in and flop down in front of a comforting plate of meatballs in tomato sauce or pasta with clams. She slept deeply in their small spare room and had a breakfast of salami, cheese and fresh crusty bread, which kept her going all day.

She meant to take them out for a treat at weekends but somehow that never worked out either. Their restaurant was so busy then, they were never free. And Helen was taking on extra classes teaching English to foreigners to meet the giant bill that she was going to have to pay to this devil travel agency. It was all very tiring, and these useless texts she got from Anthony made things worse.

At least Rosie had calmed down a bit since she had gone to London. She didn't spend all her time attacking Ronan like she normally did. She didn't complain about her high heels hurting her legs, and she said that London was very different.

She said that in every text. Helen was getting fed up with this word.

Anthony said home was different, and Rosie said London was different.

In her own life Helen found that things were just the same, with better breakfasts than back home, but the same problems about there being no men about that a sane woman would fancy. But why was everyone so busy talking about everything being different?

Helen sighed.

It would be wonderful to be in love like Maud and Marco were. They hardly had eyes for anyone else. They would laugh together and stroke each other in the restaurant kitchen before going out and being very professional in front of the customers. Back in the flat they would cuddle up together on a very small sofa and mumble at each other. Helen would go out sometimes and give them space; they were too polite to disappear and leave her there alone. It must be great to want somebody that much, Helen thought. So far in her life there had been nothing like that.

There were texts from Maud's twin brother Simon. Maud would read them out.

Simon wrote of the rave reviews they had gathered in the restaurant where he worked. There were fancy groups who came in – politicians, film stars, business people. He told of the recipes that had been a huge success, how they used seasonal ingredients, and how they had bookings six months ahead.

'He sounds very cheerful,' Helen said.

Helen had known Simon, of course, as he had grown up just down the street. He was more serious than Maud, a bit intense, she thought, but then he'd gone abroad and she hadn't seen him since.

'He has a very good job,' Marco said approvingly.

'He's lonely as hell,' Maud said firmly.

'But look at all he says about how well he's doing.' Helen was puzzled.

'A sign he's homesick.' Maud was very sure.

'Well, no point in his coming back here at the moment,' Helen said briskly. 'Restaurants are closing at one a week or is it one a day?' She looked at the stricken faces of Maud and Marco. 'Not yours, of course,' she said, too eagerly and too late.

The light had gone out of the evening.

Text from Rosie to Anthony and Helen:

I've been a week in London. The course is good and we learn a lot. It's over at six. They don't go for coffee or a drink or anything. Most of them live miles and miles away. I go back to the hotel. They allow me so much a day for my meals. I feel a bit silly in the dining room by myself every night so I have room service instead. You can't go to the bar 'cos people think you are a hooker. It's a bit odd. I read my notes. I watch telly. It wasn't really meant to be like this, was it?

Love, Rosie

Text from Anthony to Helen and Rosie:

Glad to hear that you are having a great time in London, Rosie, and that you are fine with Maud and Marco, Helen. I have been very much out of things here. It's not that Mam and Dad have gone off me or anything it's just as if I am someone who came in from the street. They seem surprised to see me every day. There's nothing to eat. They say, 'Oh are you going to use the washing machine?' as if I were going to fly to the moon. I get the sense that they are looking at my room. That Lily keeps saying that all the girls who nurse with her would just love to live in our house. I can't think why. I have a few friends who are going to live in a big flat. I think I might well join them.

Wish I had better news to pass on.

Love, Anthony

Text from Helen to Rosie and Anthony:

I never thought I'd say this but I miss the pair of you. There's a whole lot of things I'm not sure about any more. Maud and her brother Simon always paid at home when they lived with their grandparents, and Marco pays his father every week for the flat. Maybe everyone does and we should have done it too? And another thing, Maud goes up every Tuesday to her grandmother and does her washing and all the ironing and they have a great old chat. We never did that for our grannies. I know we didn't live with them. But we never did it for Mam and Dad. The people in the staffroom all live in their parents' houses and they all pay something. I'm just saying that in case you think we should offer something. What do you think?

Love, Helen

Miss Mason told Dee that Lily was more than satisfied with her new lodgings.

'Yes, it's perfect in almost every way,' Dee said. 'There's just one thing that worries me. You see, we never told our children that once they started working they should contribute at home, so they didn't. And I started to get all bitter about having to work so hard while they just sat there and ate us out of house and home. They expected *me* to have got milk for their breakfast and *me* to iron their clothes, and *me* to fill the fridge with all kinds of food for them to eat at any time of the day or the night. And now there's a bit of bad feeling.'

'You mean about Lily's room?' Miss Mason asked.

'That's only part of it. It was time to make a move, it was a hopeless state of affairs. Rosie had to go to England to do a course – and anyway she should go back to that fellow she married. And Helen's always going on about her friends Maud and Marco who apparently live the perfect life. And someone needed to wake Anthony up to the real world. But I do have regrets. If, years ago, I had asked them all for a contribution every Friday, the house could have run properly and we could have gone on forever.'

'Would you like me to find a new place for Lily so you can give back their room to the girls?' asked Miss Mason.

'No, that's not what it's about. I love Lily being there, and now that Anthony is going, Lily's friend Angela is coming to take the other room. But I'm uneasy about it. I threw out my own children and took in two strangers who pay good money. It looks as if I'm mean and grasping.'

'You're far from that.'

'But I am at fault, Miss Mason. I never asked them, you see. I know they should have known to give something – but they didn't, and their father kept saying it was their home.'

'Don't get upset, Dee. Just make us more tea and we'll sit down and see if we can work this out.' Miss Mason loved solving problems. This was a difficult one, for sure. 'The thing is, you'll have to do more than just make your children leave. That way, they'll learn nothing. You'll have to show them how things *should* have been, by how they are *now* . . .'

Chapter Seven

When Dee got back home to St Jarlath's Crescent, her son-in-law Ronan was sitting having coffee with Lily.

Lily immediately leaped up to take Dee's parcels and welcome her back to her own home. Rosie wouldn't have raised her face from a magnifying mirror; Helen's eyes would have remained glued to whatever project she was involved in. Anthony would have smiled at her from under his earphones. Before Lily, nobody was interested in Dee's day. And because Lily was so interested, Ronan was interested too.

'How would you cook those leeks, Mrs Nolan?' he asked.

Dee looked at him. Why had Rosie taken such a dislike to the boy? He seemed perfectly reasonable to Dee. Ordinary, perhaps, interested in football and pints, but then Rosie had known all this about him, so it didn't come out of a clear blue sky.

'I'd put them in a dish, cover them with

crème fraîche and heat them for half an hour. Then I'd add some grated cheese and bread-crumbs and cook them for another quarter of an hour.'

'Sounds very nice,' Ronan said.

'Yes, well, I only got enough for Liam and myself, but if you'd like to try some . . .'

'Aw, no, you're all right, Mrs Nolan, I was just wondering, that's all.'

'And do you cook for yourself these days?'

'Not really. I get chips on the way home or a Chinese or something.'

He looked sad and lonely, but Dee steeled her heart. She must not interfere. That was the rule. All her friends told her, say nothing to either of them. They'll do what they want anyway and you will be the worst in the world if you give any view at all. Keep nodding and smiling and say nothing.

Lily poured more coffee for everyone.

'I was just asking Lily here if she had any advice about what's wrong with Rosie and me,' Ronan said, 'and she doesn't know what it's all about either.' He looked puzzled.

'I was just saying it's something he and Rosie should talk about together,' Lily explained.

'Except she's in London,' Ronan said.

'I'd say she's quite lonely over there,' Lily suggested.

'Oh no, she's not, she's got all these people on a course. Anyway, Rosie would never be lonely, anywhere.'

Lily shrugged her shoulders. 'It's amazing how lonely a big city can be,' she said.

Like a light bulb over his head, Ronan was having a thought. 'Perhaps if I went over there . . .' he began.

'Well, of course, if you happened to be there . . .' Dee said neutrally.

'And you wouldn't really know how she was unless you saw her . . .' Lily continued.

Ronan stood up. 'I might have to be in London next week anyway,' he said.

The women nodded in agreement and he was gone.

'What was their falling-out about?' Lily asked.

'If I knew that, I would be a wise woman. All I know is Rosie's list of complaints. He was working too hard, he was out all hours, he wanted his shirts ironed, he didn't think much of Rosie's job. Oh, a list of things as long as your arm. None of them important. It just wasn't the fairy tale she expected.'

'So they might get back together?' Lily was hoping for a happy ending.

'They will, of course, when they have driven the rest of us demented over it all,' Dee sighed.

'But will she want her room back?' Lily wondered.

'She will be reminded that her room has been let, but she knows this already.'

'I don't like to—'

'It's got nothing to do with you, Lily.' Dee was firm. 'But I do want you to help me. I want to have a nice lunch here on Sunday and invite Helen and Anthony and Ronan, and yourself and Angela as well.'

Text to Rosie from Anthony:

Mam's invited me to lunch on Sunday, and Helen and, I believe, Ronan too. Do you think she's tired of the awful Lily and Angela? Yes, that's the new one, she's in my room. The new place I'm in is fine but the sink is full of washing-up and no one ever takes out the rubbish. Will tell you about Sunday.
   Love, Anthony

Text to Rosie from Helen:

Things look a bit more cheerful on the travel agency front. I may not owe quite as much as I feared. Bit of a mood here at the moment. When I told Maud and Marco about it I thought they'd be pleased, but Marco said it would be great that I'd have enough money to pay them rent now. And Maud just looked at the carpet. I took out a handful of euros and said, 'OK then, how much,' but Maud said we were to leave it to later when everyone was calmer. All this time they had been thinking of me as a tenant not a friend. Mam has asked us to lunch on Sunday. I don't know why, but I'm going anyway, just to try and give these two here a bit of space. I think she said Ronan is going too.

Love, Helen

Text from Ronan to Rosie:

I'm not stalking you. I have to be in London Monday evening, so maybe we could go out to dinner. Or something. Up to you. I'd love it, personally. I've been invited to your place by your mam and dad for lunch on Sunday. She texted me and invited me. It was a real invitation. It's not just that I'm hanging around there. Just so as you'd know.

Love, Ronan

Text from Rosie to Ronan:

Well, that's a lie for a start. Mam doesn't text, she doesn't know how. She said her fingers are too big. Why should I see you? Give me one good reason.
  Rosie

Sunday was a lonely day in London. Everyone else seemed to have something to do, somewhere to go.

Everyone except Rosie.

If Ronan was coming to London why couldn't he have made it on a Sunday? What business did the company have that meant he had to be in London? Why was Mam having this lunch party? Rosie wished she could be there. She felt a great hollow empty feeling in her stomach.

Is this what they meant by being homesick?

With Lily's help the kitchen had been transformed. A lick of paint here, a window-box there, and smart paper napkins on the table.

There was even a bottle of sherry – something not known in the Nolan household before this. Dee had been about to buy some wine.

82

'Surely the children will bring some?' Lily said.

'I wouldn't count on it,' Dee said.

Lily had some emergency wine in her room, just in case.

The leg of lamb was roasting in the oven. The salads were mixed. Dee was wearing her good dark dress with a pink silk rose pinned to it. Liam had put on a jacket, which he rarely did at home. Everything was ready.

Helen arrived first.

Just as she had been setting out, Maud had given her a bottle of wine to take.

'They won't expect it, it's only lunch in the kitchen as usual,' Helen said.

'It's nice to give them a surprise then,' Maud had said.

Helen handed over the bottle as she took in the whole room. It looked very different, more space somehow.

'This is very expensive wine,' her father said.

Helen tried not to look surprised. 'You're worth it,' she said. She must remember to thank Maud when she got home. It had been a perfect thing to bring.

Ronan had brought a tin of shortbread; Angela, a tall girl with curly black hair and huge glasses that magnified her eyes, brought some cheese and grapes. Lily had brought a potted plant.

Only Anthony arrived without a gift. He realised he was the only one who had turned up empty-handed.

'I'm sorry, Mam, I meant to get something,' he said fumbling a bit.

'Never mind,' Dee said briskly. 'Another time, maybe?'

'Yes, Mam.' He was confused by her, she seemed to have changed. He looked towards his father to get him out of this.

'You know how it is, Da?' he said.

'Yes, your mother's quite right, it will do another time,' Dad said pleasantly.

Anthony looked at him in dismay. This was Da, for heaven's sake. What had happened here?

Liam carved the lamb; everyone said it was gorgeous. Well, Angela and Lily said it over and over, and gradually Anthony and Helen got pulled into the hymn of praise.

'It's so lovely to get a whole joint roasted properly,' Angela said.

'There's always a joint in this house on a Sunday,' Dee said.

Helen and Anthony looked at each other bewildered. Was there a joint every Sunday?

Helen tried to think back. Yes, maybe her mother had roasted something on Sundays. Helen had never cared really, just sat down and eaten it like any other day. There had never been fuss and paper napkins and sherry and everyone bringing presents before. But that was just to impress the lodgers.

Helen longed to know how much the nurses were paying Mam a week. But she couldn't ask. Maybe Rosie knew. She'd text her and ask her later. Meanwhile she must ask tactfully when she could go to her room and collect some more clothes. Things were so difficult these days, you had to walk on eggshells. Like you couldn't mention unemployment because of Dad, or holidays because Mam and Dad had never had one. Actually you couldn't talk about anything at all because Mam seemed to have invented a new family with these two nurses. They were OK of course and very polite, but they kept fawning over the house in St Jarlath's Crescent as if it was some kind of stately home.

'Mam, I hope it will be convenient for me to get some clothes,' she began when the meal was finally over.

'Any time you want, love, but have you a bag with you to carry them?' Mam seemed perfectly happy about it.

'But will that be OK with you, Lily? I mean, it's sort of your room now.'

'Oh, they're not in Lily's room, your clothes are out in the back kitchen.' Mam seemed surprised at the thought that Helen should want to go to her own room.

'Out at the back? In the damp?' she cried out, shocked and disbelieving. 'Dad, did you hear what Mam's done with my clothes?'

'It's hardly damp, Helen, I've put plenty of good heating in it.'

'It's like a coal-hole,' she wailed.

'Not now it's not,' her father said.

Helen leaped from the table and went to the little scullery. It had been totally transformed, the walls painted white, with red and white curtains at the window. A sofa bed with a scarlet cover stood against one wall and three clothes rails by the other. Helen saw the one marked with her name, her dresses, blouses and skirts all hanging neatly on wire clothes hangers. Under the rail were boxes, all of them with her name painted on them. Shoes and underwear, she supposed.

But it was so final. All these things had been

taken from her room and brought down here without her permission. And after Dad always saying, 'This is your home'. She stared around the room in disbelief.

There was a rail and a set of boxes for Anthony and Rosie too. They were going to feel like she felt, wounded and upset. She came back to the table where they were all still sitting laughing at some story Ronan was telling them.

'You didn't take anything?' Mam said, surprised.

'When did all this happen?' Helen asked in a frosty voice.

If Dee noticed her tone she showed no signs of it.

'Oh, we've spent the last two weeks doing it. Your father has been worked off his feet.'

'Well, as long as you all like it, it's worth it,' he said with what Helen thought was a foolish smile.

'But why did you do it?' Helen's eyes were cold.

'Well, we thought it was nice to have another bedroom in case any of you needed a bed from time to time.' Dee seemed pleased to be talking about the room. 'And we thought the red and white was good, cheerful and everything.'

'But all the rails of clothes . . . ?' Helen

couldn't get any kind of a grip on what was happening.

'I know they're a bit in your face at the moment but when you have all taken your clothes away, then it will be a proper spare room. Your dad is going to make a dressing table with little lights around the mirror.'

'When we have all taken all our clothes away?' Helen repeated bleakly.

'To your *own* places,' Dee explained as if she were talking to someone of very low understanding.

'But we haven't *got* our own places!' Helen looked wildly at Anthony for support. He just seemed to be equally confused.

'Are my things in there too?' he asked.

'Yes, love, to make room for Angela,' his mother reassured him.

'I won't fit all my things into the lads' flat.' Anthony was worried.

'Well, maybe you should get a bigger place,' his mother said.

'But how would I afford that?'

'I suppose you could go out and get some work . . .' Dee was bright and helpful.

'What about Rosie's things?' Ronan was anxious.

'When she comes back from London, I'm

sure she'll have made up her mind about where she wants to go. I mean, it was always temporary for her coming back here.'

'I wonder does she realise that,' Ronan muttered.

'Of course she does. Anyway you can always tell her when you are in London.'

'I think I'll keep quiet on this one, Mrs Nolan. There's so much else to discuss.'

'Certainly, Ronan, you'll know what's best.' Dee smiled at him.

There was something about her that said lunch was not over. Helen was about to slink off to brood about it all when Lily, with her voice like a clear bell, said, 'That was such a lovely meal, why don't you two sit down and we'll clear it all away?'

Dee accepted, delighted. She and Liam sat down eagerly in their two big chairs. Ronan was placed in charge of saucepans, oven dishes and general greasy things; Anthony and Helen found themselves doing the drying as the two nurses washed everything. Then the teacloths were washed and laid out on a radiator.

Anthony went glumly to examine the back room. Helen joined him as he stood there looking at it all in amazement.

'Imagine them doing this,' Helen said.

'They're throwing us out,' Anthony said. 'You do realise what's happening? They are actually throwing us out of our own home!'

Chapter Eight

Next morning, Ronan flew to London. He had had terrible trouble getting the two days off work. He ended up telling his boss that this was make or break time in his marriage.

'And how will your having two days off help?' his boss asked.

'I don't know,' Ronan admitted. 'But I think it will.'

'It's an expensive thing for me, your going off to another country.' The boss was still unconvinced, but he gave in. Ronan was to be back first thing on Wednesday morning. 'OK?'

'OK,' Ronan agreed.

One night and two days. He hoped it would work. Rosie was The One. It was just that she was a bit shrill and had ideas of what a marriage should be. Fine ideas if you didn't have to earn a living . . .

Ronan took an early flight and looked at the businessmen with their briefcases and some businesswomen too. Studying files, getting themselves ready for some meeting or other. Well-dressed, finely groomed, people of power. He envied them their confidence. They would have been able to sort this thing out with Rosie in two minutes.

He got the underground from the airport into central London and began to look for a good place for lunch. Rosie was going to give up her afternoon lecture so that they could talk. He needed to find a place that was romantic and attractive, not somewhere they would be barked at and their plates snatched away. He headed towards Covent Garden as he had heard it was romantic and nice to walk around. He found a place with vines all over it, which looked just right. Then he saw the prices on the menu. The cost of one starter was greater than Ronan had ever paid for any meal for two. He moved swiftly on.

He finally found a small Italian place that he could afford.

'I am inviting someone to lunch and it may go on a long time,' Ronan said.

'Signor . . . I ask you, when the good God made time, did he not make plenty of it? What is life if we do not have enough time? You stay as long as you like.'

Ronan stood there, stunned.

That was it.

Time.

That was what was missing in their lives. That was at the root of it all. He booked the table and called his wife.

'I've found a lovely Italian restaurant for lunch,' he said.

'Will you want to go out to eat again tonight?' she asked.

'Why don't we wait and see? We have plenty of time. You know, I was thinking, what is life if we don't have enough time?'

'That's a bit of a change of direction for you,' Rosie said.

'See you at one-thirty,' Ronan said.

Text from Anthony to Rosie:

You asked me to tell you about the lunch. It was weird. That's what it was. We were all meant to bring presents like a birthday. It's as if she's adopted those two, Lily and Angela. They're her new family. But, wait for it, she and Da have painted up the scullery all red and white, with a bed in it in case any of us ever need a bed overnight, and they've put all our clothes on rails and in boxes. It's like a posh left-luggage place. Come home soon,

Rosie. You might make some sense out of it all.

Love, Anthony

Text to Rosie from Helen:

They have both gone utterly mad. All our clothes are in the back kitchen. They talk about us all 'finding our own places'. I thought we had *found our own place and it was at home. Why have they changed? Was it Dad losing his job? Or Mam getting the change of life? Whatever it is, it's not good. Wish you were at home. You might understand.*

Love, Helen

Rosie read the two texts and was pleased to think the others thought she would understand what was going on, but at the same time she felt relieved that she wasn't there. She wished she could talk to Mam about this meeting with Ronan. Mam didn't say much but she listened, and somehow it straightened things out, just having her there listening.

Mam didn't really understand why Rosie had left Ronan. She used to say things like 'You used to love him' or 'When did you stop loving him?' That wasn't what it was all about;

it was about the empty evenings, and Ronan coming in dog-tired, and the ironing. All that ironing.

If Mam couldn't understand, and Ronan was blind to it all, how was there any way of making things better?

And now it seemed as if Mam and Dad had gone right round the bend and she had no home to go back to either.

Dee was finishing up at Miss Mason's apartment. She looked at her watch and sighed. Just about now Ronan and Rosie would be meeting for lunch. It would probably end up as a screaming match. Or, rather, Rosie screaming and Ronan shrugging his shoulders and saying he didn't know what it was all about. He didn't go with other women, he didn't get drunk and abusive – would she *like* him to do these things?

Such a waste, Dee thought to herself. Two young people who should be building up a home and having a family.

But then having a family wasn't all a bed of roses. Dee had seen the faces of her son and daughter yesterday when she had shown them their clothes all neatly stacked waiting to be taken away. She felt very guilty, and could hardly sleep, thinking about it. The guilt was not that she was making her children leave home. It was that she hadn't done it sooner or made an arrangement with them that they needed to pay something towards their keep. *That* had been her great mistake.

If she had her life over again, she would have made all this very clear to them from the start.

It was very harsh to move the goalposts for them so suddenly and Dee felt bad about it. She was muttering to herself when Miss Mason asked what she was saying.

'A sort of prayer, I think.'

'You don't need to pray, you're a saint already, or so Lily says. Didn't the lunch work out perfectly yesterday?'

'It went fine. Everyone seemed to enjoy it but Anthony and Helen were a bit shell-shocked.'

'You invited them again for next Sunday?'

'Yes. I told them we would be having beef, but I don't think it's enough, Miss Mason.'

'Enough?'

'To make up for throwing them out. Yes, that's the way they see it. They are being thrown out of their own home. Oh I do *wish* that I had handled it differently. Told them that life was tough and you have to go out and work for money.' Dee looked very miserable.

'Oh, Dee, come on now. You have everything

going fine, stop worrying, and think about the next part of our plan, to get work for Liam. Do you have those little cards?'

Dee handed over the little cards they had got printed. They had Liam's name and mobile phone number and the fact that he was a reliable, fully qualified electrician who had worked many years for the same firm in the building trade. This would let people know he could be trusted, that he wasn't a cowboy. Or that was what they hoped.

'I'll bring the subject up at my bridge session this afternoon,' Miss Mason said. 'And tomorrow, when I'm at the Residents' Association meeting. There has to be *someone* there who needs plugs changed or a new television set tuned in.'

'You are very good, Miss Mason,' Dee said from the heart.

'No, actually, I'm not good but I am tough and that helps a lot in life.'

'But I don't want to win by scoring over my children,' Dee said.

'No, no, that's not what you are about. But you *do* want to keep an eye on them and make them feel welcome. That's why we decided on these Sunday lunches.'

'I wish I could believe they will work,' Dee sighed.

Helen was in the school staffroom eating a sandwich. There was always plenty of food in Marco and Maud's kitchen: she just took some more slices of salami and cheese and a bap. It saved paying for lunch.

Her mobile phone rang; it was the travel agency. It had all been sorted, there had been an insurance policy written into the agreement, Helen was off the hook. She felt a huge weight rise from her shoulders, and suddenly she was able to breathe properly again.

Helen was longing to tell someone.

She couldn't say anything to her colleagues. They had all said she was mad in the first place to promise the children a holiday that she could not deliver.

She didn't want to tell Mam and Dad. They would advise her to open a proper savings' account, to be sensible and to get a mortgage on a house.

But she did need a nice party frock to go out and celebrate, so she set out for St Jarlath's Crescent to pick something up from her rail. Helen still had her own key. At least Mam had not asked for them back yet.

Just outside the house Helen met Fiona Carroll, Dr Declan's wife. She herself was a nurse, and always had a word for everyone.

Helen wondered about Fiona's life. She worked hard up at the hospital. She had two small children *and* her husband worked all the hours God sent – but she never moaned and grizzled about it like Rosie did. She always seemed happy and today she had one baby in a pram and a toddler running beside her. Helen couldn't remember if the new baby was a boy or a girl, she must be careful not to say the wrong name.

'Hi, Helen,' Fiona greeted her. 'I haven't seen you around for a while. Your mam said you were sharing a flat with friends.'

'Yeah, sort of,' Helen said.

'It's good to have all that freedom, isn't it?' Fiona asked.

'Sure, in a way. It's different, though.'

'I know, and it can be expensive having your own place.'

'Well, it can be, certainly.'

'How much do you pay a week?' Fiona asked, interested.

'That's hard to say,' Helen stumbled.

'Sorry, maybe you think I'm pushy. It's just

my friend Barbara's letting a room and she doesn't know what to charge.'

'I'm their guest at the moment,' Helen said in a burst of honesty.

'Oh – that's nice.' Fiona seemed startled.

'Fiona, did you pay your mother and father when you lived with them?' Helen asked.

'Well, yes, once I started to work, of course I did, every week. They put it in a savings account for me. And it added up. They gave it all back to me on my wedding day. I cried my eyes out . . .'

'And your friend, Barbara, did she pay at home?'

'What is this, Helen? Of course she did. Everyone does.'

'Sure. I was just checking that's all . . .'

And Helen went glumly into the house where she and her sister and brother had never paid one cent towards living expenses.

Rosie and Ronan were sitting contentedly in the restaurant, watching the busy lunch trade of business people and tourists. They sipped a cold white wine and ate pasta. It was like the old days.

They talked easily, there was no confrontation.

'Tell me about the scullery that they've painted white,' she said.

'It looks great, like a real room. Your clothes are all there hanging on a rail.'

'They'd better be there,' Rosie muttered darkly.

'I asked your mam and dad why hadn't they ever done it up before.'

'What did they say?'

'They said they couldn't afford to before.'

'So how can they afford it now? Did they win the lotto?'

'No, Rosie, they got some rent for the first time. It made all the difference.'

There was a little silence between them.

'That was a good question to ask,' Rosie said grudgingly.

'Maybe you should have . . . we should have . . .'

'Don't tell me now, when it's all too late,' Rosie said.

'I was hoping it's not too late for us,' he said.

'What?'

'I will iron my own shirts, whatever way you like, once a week, once a night, whatever suits you. I'll insist I have at least two nights a week where I do not go out at all and two more where I get home by eight . . .'

She looked at him silently.

'I don't know what exactly I'm doing wrong that's upsetting you so much, Rosie. Honestly I don't. If I say I love you, you say it's just words. If I don't say I love you, then you say I'm cold and unfeeling. Remember when we were first together? You loved me then . . .'

'I know,' she said in a small voice.

'So is there anything I could do to make it right again?'

Rosie looked at him for what seemed a long time. She reached across the table and held both his hands.

'You did it. You made up all that business about having to do some work in London, you put your job at risk and came over to see me.'

Ronan still wasn't sure. She was smiling and had tears in her eyes but that could mean anything.

'So this means . . . ?' He stopped and waited.

'It means I'm coming home, Ronan.'

Anthony was not a fusspot, he said, but really and truly the lads' place was filthy. The bath had a black ring around it, and the kitchen was filled with the empty or nearly empty containers of takeaway food. If they missed bin night, which happened regularly, it meant that this rubbish could hang around for two weeks.

Anthony found himself filling black bags every Tuesday just to keep the place from becoming a fever pit. They were a great bunch of guys and there was music day and night. But there was also a lot of smoking, a lot of drinking and very late nights.

He remembered the clean kitchen back home in St Jarlath's Crescent. When they had that lunch there with the roast lamb and things, it had all seemed like a high-class restaurant compared to where he was living now. And he was completely broke from buying food and drink. Amazingly, all the other lads had paid something at home. He never had. Maybe that's why Mam had thrown them out.

He had a job two nights a week, collecting glasses in a pub. Not real money, but enough to pay something, if that's what it was all about.

He needed to get his head clear.

It was hard to do with the fumes coming from the kitchen.

Helen found her party frock, and left a note for Mam on the kitchen table, thanking her again for the lovely Sunday lunch. Then she went and bought a bottle of champagne to take back to Maud and Marco's.

As soon as she opened the door, she told them that she wanted to celebrate the fact that she wasn't bankrupt and to ask them what they considered a fair rent for her stay. She didn't get to the end of her sentence as they cried they had something to celebrate too. Maud's twin brother Simon had come back for a visit.

And there he was, the boy she remembered from years back, but not serious and tense as he used to be. He was relaxed and tanned and . . . well . . . glorious.

'Hello, Simon,' she said, feeling that any minute she might faint.

'Helen, you look terrific,' he said, smiling at her.

Maud and Marco looked at each other in surprise.

It had actually happened. Simon had at last met a girl he was interested in. Even though it was their troubled, tight-fisted tenant, she *was* a girl . . .

Chapter Nine

Then everything began to move very quickly indeed.

Dee told Josie that it was like when they turned on fast forward in a video. People were running in and out of the house all the time. It was impossible to keep up.

Ronan came back from London with a great smile on his face and began to collect Rosie's clothes from the rail in the back room. Dee watched while he lovingly packed Rosie's shoes in boxes and her handbags into clear plastic bags. He asked Dee for lessons in ironing and watched gravely as she showed him how to position the collars.

'There's more to it than I thought,' he said.

Dee actually felt that there was *less* to it than anyone thought, but wisely said nothing.

Ronan also asked her how to make a good casserole. 'I want to spend quality time with Rosie in the kitchen,' he said.

Again, Dee wondered why on earth he should want this, but patiently showed him how to make a few simple dishes. He was as grateful as if he had been given the deeds of a house.

Anthony asked her advice about clearing up a very dirty flat. Dee offered to go and help him on the premises, but he said no, if she did that once they would expect it all the time. So she listed some detergents and disinfectants as well as cleaning materials. She suggested that he get a few big buckets and line them with black bags and that he make a list of who did what.

'They wouldn't take any notice, Mam.'

'Then you could live with different people maybe?'

'I *like* them, Mam, we play great music – it's just that they don't seem to notice the state of the place. What do you think I should do?'

'I know what you *should* do, which is what I told you already. Just once. Clean it, sort out the cleaning rota, and they could well be so pleased they'll keep it that way.'

'But you see, Mam—' he began.

'I know, Anthony, I know they might get annoyed with you . . . There might be a lot of fuss, it's kind of easier to leave things the way they are.'

He was surprised that she understood. Then a thought came to him.

'Was that the way it was with us, when we all lived here?' he asked.

'A bit like that, yes. Why disturb things? Anything for an easy life.'

'And what changed it?'

'I don't know. Not any one thing. Just a feeling, you know, that it was *always* going to be like this. No milk in the fridge, no one doing anything, no one paying anything, and me getting more bitter and twisted every day. I had thought it would be different, a bit shinier somehow.'

'Sorry, Mam.'

'No, it was all my fault. And if you let those guys live in filth around you, then it's *your* fault. That's all I'm saying.'

'What's the best thing for burned saucepans, Mam?' he asked.

'Cooking over a low heat and taking the pan off on time,' she said.

'I mean the ones that are burned already,' he said, sadly.

'Wire wool and a scourer,' Dee suggested.

Anthony listened as if this was divine wisdom.

'You're great, Mam,' he said.

'I am,' Dee said happily. 'That's what I am, I'm great.'

*

Helen came back with all her clothes.

'I don't want my old room back, Mam,' she said immediately.

'No, indeed,' Dee said.

'But you *did* say something about the bed in the scullery—'

'The back room,' Dee corrected.

'Yes, whatever. You *did* say that if we were ever stuck we could have a few nights there.'

'And you are stuck?' Dee enquired.

'Not really, it's just that I want Maud and Marco to have more space, and, you see, Maud's brother Simon came home . . .'

'You mentioned that all right,' Dee said.

'And I wouldn't want him to think that I was . . . you know, settling in on them or anything.'

'No, indeed.' Dee nodded gravely. 'Settling in on people would look bad all right.'

Something about the way she said it made Helen look at her mother's face. She could find nothing to help her there, it made her slightly uneasy.

'I mean, I wouldn't exactly be settling in, when I sleep in the scullery,' Helen said defensively.

'Back room,' Dee corrected automatically.

'Er . . . yes of course, the back room,' Helen said.

'So how long will you need it for?' Dee was perfectly polite, hospitable even, but there was certainly a time limit hovering in the air.

'About a week if that's all right.'

'That should be fine. I'll check with your dad.'

'I'll check,' Helen offered.

Dad was out in his shed working on an old radio that was of huge sentimental value to someone in Miss Mason's apartment block. He looked up, pleased, when he saw Helen.

'Great to see you, love, and how are the little monsters?'

'They're not monsters, Dad, they're great. Full of imagination and hopes and dreams. I love them.'

'You're great when you talk about teaching.' Liam Nolan sounded genuinely admiring. 'You're a different person.'

'Different from what?' Helen wondered.

'Well, you know, fussing and complaining about money and everything.'

'It's just I don't have any money to speak of,' Helen said.

'None of us have any money to *speak* of, love,

but we manage, and we don't go on about it, you know.'

Helen was stunned.

Did she go on about it? No, of course she didn't. It was just all that business about the travel agency.

Then she remembered something Marco had said about money recently and how Maud had changed the subject.

Rosie and Anthony had often accused her of being Miss Moneybox, but that was just the way families go on.

At school they used to make fun of her bringing in sandwiches instead of going out to the little pasta restaurant with the rest of them.

But Helen actually winced when she thought of Simon saying that he was sure Maud and Marco would be sorry to lose their lodger. He probably thought she paid rent.

She felt her face and neck reddening at the thought he might ever find out.

'Yes, I see what you mean,' she said sadly to her father.

'It's not important, Helen . . .' He always hated any kind of tension. 'I mean, that was all a misunderstanding in the past. You all know now what it costs to run a house and how your poor mother has been working way too hard to make life easy for everyone.'

'Yes, Dad. And Dad, I was wondering if I could stay in the scullery – the back room – for a week from now, like . . .'

'Your mother will deal that,' he said.

'She said she wanted to check with you first.' Helen looked at him hopefully.

'Well, I'm not sure exactly. I'm not great with figures and money, but there's no way you should pay as much for the back room as for a proper bedroom. Will we say half of what Lily and Angela pay? Would that be all right? Is that fair?'

Helen swallowed. She was going to have to *pay* to stay in the scullery? Had the world gone mad? But she had to stay somewhere. And soon.

'Of course, Dad, that sounds totally fair,' she managed to say and let him get back to the elderly radio.

Ronan had flowers on the dining table, he had the casserole ready to put into the oven, and the salad already prepared in the fridge. He had ironed all Rosie's dresses and hung them carefully in the bedroom so that she would notice how smooth and uncrushed they were. Then he went to the airport.

He had a speech ready but when she threw herself into his arms, he forgot the speech entirely.

'Welcome home,' was all he said.

In Anthony's house, the musicians were staring in amazement at the kitchen. They wondered were they in the right house.

The kitchen was gleaming, and a big bin stood clean and lined, awaiting rubbish. Crockery and glasses were washed and put away. Surfaces were gleaming and bare. The sink was empty and shining.

Most menacing of all was a clipboard. There were four people in the house, so there were duties that had to be done every day. They needed discussing.

In order to lessen the shock, Anthony revealed that he had ordered fish and chips to be delivered later in the evening and worked out what each person should pay.

They were defiant at first. Anthony was turning out to be worse than their mothers, they said.

Then they saw the sense in it. They could

112

even bring women home to a place as classy as this, they agreed.

The deal was done.

'We will miss you,' Marco said to Helen.

'I want to settle up with you for my time here,' Helen said. She tried to take the note of horror out of her voice. She hoped she did not look too pleading, too begging for them to say that she owed them nothing.

'Let's see, it was four weeks, wasn't it?' Marco said.

'But mates' rates,' Maud insisted. 'Not real money, just enough to cover a few things.'

They settled on a sum.

It was very reasonable for four weeks' board and lodging, but if you had expected to pay nothing, like Helen had, it was fairly substantial. She smiled and chattered her way through it. Then Simon came in and said he would love to help her carry her things back to her house in St Jarlath's Crescent.

'It's only temporary there,' Helen said.

'I know. Maybe you could get a flat in Chestnut Court. They're very nice,' Simon said.

'They're very expensive,' Helen blurted out before she could help herself.

'Well, between two they mightn't be too bad,' Simon said.

'Two?'

'Well, I can't settle on Marco and Maud forever. I'll need a place of my own too. We might share the experience. What do you think?'

'What a great idea,' Helen said with a big wide smile.

Dee made Simon very welcome. They talked about his grandmother Lizzie who lived down the road, and about his wonderful grandfather, Muttie, who had died and left a great ache in the street. They remembered Hooves the faithful dog who had died just hours before his master.

They got on very well, Helen noticed, easy and relaxed. Not tense like she had been with her mother. But she didn't really concentrate on what they were saying.

Simon had asked her to share a flat with him. *Imagine.*

By the time the twenty-fifth wedding anniversary came, everything had settled down.

Rosie was the happiest wife in Dublin. She and Ronan came every Sunday to lunch in St Jarlath's Crescent, where nowadays they were joined by Simon who was very much together with Helen, and Babette, who was a saxophonist much fancied by Anthony.

Nobody used the back room now, so Lily and Angela had installed yet another nurse in there. The rent coming in was substantial. It had all been saved carefully in the post office, and would be spent on a holiday in Sicily.

But first there was a party.

It was in Ennio's, the restaurant belonging to Marco's father. All kinds of people were there: Miss Mason, of course, and Josie and Harry, and half of St Jarlath's Crescent. Anthony's girlfriend Babette was dressed as a Goth.

Liam and Dee had to make speeches, of course. Everyone else had toasted them and said what a wonderful couple they were and how they had done everything right all their life.

This was so far from being true, but at a party, in the middle of a celebration, people did not want to hear of the hard times, the mistakes made and the wrong turnings taken.

They spoke simply of the life they had lived and the joy of their three children. It had been a happy home, but then, like in every home, just as the leaves fall from the trees, the children had left to set up lives for themselves and this was a source of great happiness to them.

They could only wish their two daughters and son as happy lives as they had lived themselves.

In the crowd, Rosie, Helen and Anthony stood there astounded. What was this Mam and Dad were saying – that their children had left *like the leaves fall gently from the tree*? That wasn't how *they* remembered it.

It had been sudden and shocking and up-setting. Mam and Dad had painted up the scullery and put all their children's clothes there. Their visits had been more or less reduced to Sunday lunch. Rent had been men-tioned in what was supposed, after all, to be their home . . .

But in the end what did it matter?

Their parents were happy and smiling. They actually *believed* all this 'leaves-falling-off-the-trees' thing. Tomorrow they were going to Sicily for two weeks.

Raise the glass, drink their health.

Maybe it had all been for the best.

Say nothing, now or any time, about the sudden dismantling of the full house. Maybe

116

the wind had needed a little help to blow the leaves off the trees.

That's all there was to it.

Quick Reads 📖

Books in the Quick Reads series

Lose yourself
in a good
book with *Galaxy®*

Curled up on the sofa,
Sunday morning in pyjamas,
just before bed,
in the bath or
on the way to work?

Wherever, whenever,
you can escape
with a good book!

So go on...
indulge yourself with
a good read and the
smooth taste of
Galaxy® chocolate.

Proud Sponsors of  **and**

Read more at facebook.com/galaxy

Quick Reads

Fall in love with reading

Quick Reads are brilliantly written short new books by bestselling authors and celebrities. Whether you're an avid reader who wants a quick fix or haven't picked up a book since school, sit back, relax and let Quick Reads inspire you.

We would like to thank all our funders:

We would also like to thank all our partners in the Quick Reads project for their help and support:

NIACE • unionlearn • National Book Tokens
The Reading Agency • National Literacy Trust
Welsh Books Council • Welsh Government
The Big Plus Scotland • DELNI • NALA

We want to get the country reading

Quick Reads, World Book Day and World Book Night are initiatives designed to encourage everyone in the UK and Ireland – whatever your age – to read more and discover the joy of books.

Quick Reads launches on **14 February 2012**
Find out how you can get involved at www.**quickreads**.org.uk

World Book Day is on **1 March 2012**
Find out how you can get involved at www.**worldbookday**.com

World Book Night is on **23 April 2012**
Find out how you can get involved at www.**worldbooknight**.org

Quick Reads 📖

Fall in love with reading

Amy's Diary

Maureen Lee

Orion

A young woman finds her way
in a world at war.

On 3rd September 1939 Amy Browning started to write
a diary. It was a momentous day: Amy's 18th birthday
and the day her sister gave birth to a baby boy. It was
also the day Great Britain went to war with Germany.

To begin with life for Amy and her family in Opal Street,
Liverpool, went on much the same. Then the bombs
began to fall, and Amy's fears grew. Her brother was
fighting in France, her boyfriend had joined the RAF and
they all now lived in a very dangerous world …

Quick Reads 📖

Fall in love with reading

The Little One

Lynda La Plante

Simon & Schuster

Are you scared of the dark?

Barbara needs a story. A struggling journalist, she tricks her way into the home of former soap star Margaret Reynolds. Desperate for a scoop, she finds instead a terrified woman living alone in a creepy manor house.
A piano plays in the night, footsteps run overhead, doors slam. The nights are full of strange noises. Barbara thinks there may be a child living upstairs, unseen. Little by little, actress Margaret's haunting story is revealed, and Barbara is left with a chilling discovery.

This spooky tale from bestselling author Lynda La Plante will make you want to sleep with the light on.

Quick Reads

Fall in love with reading

Doctor Who
Magic of the Angels

Jacqueline Rayner

BBC Books

'No one from this time
will ever see that girl again . . .'

On a sight-seeing tour of London the Doctor wonders why so many young girls are going missing. When he sees Sammy Star's amazing magic act, he thinks he knows the answer. The Doctor and his friends team up with residents of an old people's home to discover the truth. And together they find themselves face to face with a deadly Weeping Angel.

Whatever you do – don't blink!

A thrilling all-new adventure featuring the Doctor, Amy and Rory, as played by Matt Smith, Karen Gillan and Arthur Darvill in the hit series from BBC Television.

Quick Reads

Fall in love with reading

Beyond the Bounty

Tony Parsons

Harper

Mutiny and murder in paradise …

The Mutiny on the Bounty is the most famous uprising in naval history. Led by Fletcher Christian, a desperate crew cast sadistic Captain Bligh adrift. They swap cruelty and the lash for easy living in the island heaven of Tahiti. However, paradise turns out to have a darker side …

Mr Christian dies in terrible agony. The Bounty burns. Cursed by murder and treachery, the rebels' dreams turn to nightmares, and all hope of seeing England again is lost forever …

Quick Reads 📖

Fall in love with reading

The Cleverness of Ladies

Alexander McCall Smith

Abacus

There are times when ladies must use
all their wisdom to tackle life's mysteries.

Mma Ramotswe, owner of the No.1 Ladies' Detective Agency, keeps her wits about her as she looks into why the country's star goalkeeper isn't saving goals. Georgina turns her rudeness into a virtue when she opens a successful hotel. Fabrizia shows her bravery when her husband betrays her. And gentle La proves that music really can make a difference.

With his trademark gift for storytelling, International bestselling author Alexander McCall Smith brings us five tales of love, heartbreak, hope and the cleverness of ladies.

Other resources

Enjoy this book? Find out about all the others from
www.quickreads.org.uk

Free courses are available for anyone who wants to develop
their skills. You can attend the courses in your local area.
If you'd like to find out more, phone 0800 66 0800.

Don't get by 0800 66 0800

For more information on developing your skills in Scotland
visit www.**thebigplus**.com

Join the Reading Agency's Six Book Challenge at
www.**sixbookchallenge**.org.uk

Publishers Barrington Stoke and New Island
also provide books for new readers.
www.**barringtonstoke**.co.uk • www.**newisland**.ie

The BBC runs an adult basic skills campaign.
See www.**bbc**.co.uk/**skillswise**

Skillswise